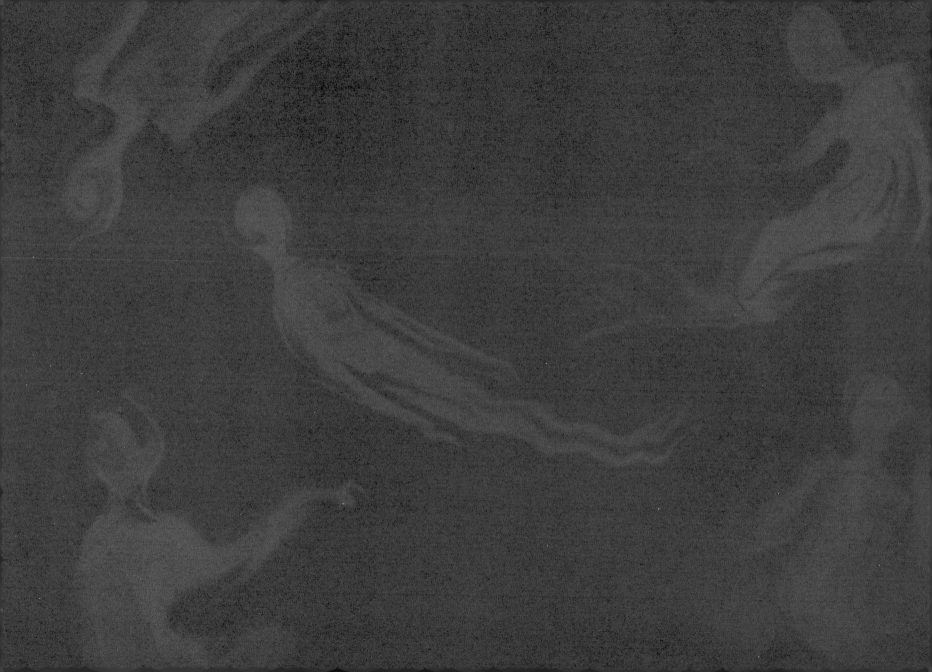

The Shaman's Apprentice

Published by Inhabit Media Inc. | www.inhabitmedia.com

Inhabit Media Inc. (Iqaluit) P.O. Box 11125, Iqaluit, Nunavut, X0A 1H0
(Toronto) 191 Eglinton Avenue East, Suite 301, Toronto, Ontario, M4P 1K1

Editors: Neil Christopher and Kelly Ward
Art Director: Danny Christopher
Designer: Astrid Arijanto

We acknowledge the support of the Canada Council for the Arts for our publishing program.
This project was made possible in part by the Government of Canada.

Library and Archives Canada Cataloguing in Publication
Title: The shaman's apprentice / by Zacharias Kunuk ; illustrated by Megan Kyak-Monteith.
Names: Kunuk, Zacharias, author. | Kyak-Monteith, Megan, illustrator.
Identifiers: Canadiana 20200351419 | ISBN 9781772272680 (hardcover)
Subjects: LCGFT: Fiction. | LCGFT: Illustrated works.
Classification: LCC PS8621.U58 S53 2021 | DDC jC813/.6—dc23

ISBN: 978-1-77227-268-0

Printed and bound in China by Hung Hing Off-set Printing Co. Ltd., December 2020, PPO#09242022

The Shaman's Apprentice

By Zacharias Kunuk

Illustrated by Megan Kyak-Monteith

Supijaq sat in the *qarmaq*, quietly sewing a skin. She was preparing a mask for her grandmother to use in an upcoming ceremony. Her grandmother, Qunguliq, sat silently tending the *qulliq* on the other sleeping platform. The only sound was that of the wind battering the outside of the qarmaq.

Suddenly, the space filled with afternoon sunlight as a young man burst in. "There is a very sick man in my camp who needs to be healed," he said.

Qunguliq raised her eyebrows. "Supijaq, take my *qurvik* and pack it on the *qamutiik*," she said as she stood to join the man.

Supijaq did as she was told and carried the pot out to the qamutiik.

Qunguliq and Supijaq travelled with the young man as fast as his dogs would take them to the next camp.
Supijaq wondered what she would see when they arrived.

As the qamutiik raced over some rough ice, the qurvik fell from the sled. Qunguliq and Supijaq did not notice it fall, as the sound of it hitting the ground behind them was carried away on the wind. The pot disappeared into the distance as they continued on.

When they arrived at the sick man's qarmaq, they could see that he was very ill. He was lying on a sleeping platform covered in skins. He was sweating and did not seem to have enough energy to move.

Qunguliq approached the man. "Do you know why you're sick? Have you done something wrong?" she asked him. "Tell me and I'll help you."

The man looked at Qunguliq, then simply turned his head, refusing to answer her.

Qunguliq narrowed her eyes and stared at the sick man for some time. Then she turned to Supijaq.

"Fetch my qurvik, Supijaq," she said.

Supijaq did as she was asked, but she did not see the qurvik. She returned and told her grandmother that the qurvik was not there.

"Nonsense," Qunguliq said. "You will find the pot outside of the qarmaq. Go get it."

Supijaq again did as she was told, knowing she had just checked outside and found nothing. And yet, the pot was right where Qunguliq said it would be.

Supijaq brought the pot to Qunguliq. Qunguliq used it, dipped her hand in the urine, and smeared the liquid on the sick man—a technique she had used before to help heal the sick.

The man continued to writhe under the skins. The urine had no effect.

Qunguliq turned to Supijaq. "It is not working," she said, gravely. "We will have to travel underground."

Qunguliq and Supijaq hung a sealskin curtain over the back wall of the qarmaq, as Qunguliq sang a magic song. When they were finished, Qunguliq lifted the curtain to reveal a deep hole leading underground. Supijaq looked at her grandmother tentatively.

"This is a dangerous place," Qunguliq said. "To go underground, you have to be ready. You cannot show fear."

Supijaq raised her eyebrows, showing that she understood. She moved to take her first step down the hole, but Qunguliq stopped her.

"Are you sure you're ready?" she asked.

Supijaq looked down into the darkness and proceeded into the hole.

The hole descended deep into the earth. Supijaq and Qunguliq moved down the slope carefully.

Suddenly, when she was about halfway down, Supijaq felt a strange sensation. Her body was changing, becoming limp and soft as her own bones seemed to leave her body. When they reached the bottom of the hole, the bodies of both Supijaq and Qunguliq consisted only of flesh.

At the bottom of the hole, Supijaq and Qunguliq found themselves in a tunnel. The walls were covered in animal hides that had paw prints on them.

The tunnel led to the entrance of an *iglu*. A massive husky lay next to the door, surrounded by the skulls and bones of humans he had recently eaten.

Supijaq looked at her grandmother. "We cannot show fear," Qunguliq whispered. "If you show fear, the dog will smell it and eat you."

Supijaq took a deep breath and stepped over the dog's tail. The dog shifted and growled quietly, sniffing the air, but Supijaq continued and passed through the entrance.

As Supijaq's vision adjusted to the dimly lit room, she saw that they were not alone in the space. Near the back of the iglu, several tormented human spirits struggled under a sheet. Closer to where Supijaq stood, an old woman tended a qulliq. Her long black hair completely obscured her face, and her caribou *amauti* had turned grey with age.

"That is Kannaaluk, The One Below," Qunguliq whispered. "She will tell us what we need to know to heal the sick man."

Supijaq and Qunguliq approached the old woman. All three were silent for a moment. Eventually the old woman began moving her hand over her body. She paused with her hand on her side before reaching inside her torso, behind her ribs, and pulling out a polar bear tongue.

As soon as Kannaaluk showed Supijaq and Qunguliq the tongue, they had a vision. They saw the sick man, healthy and stalking a polar bear across the sea ice. As soon as he had caught the bear, the man cut out the tongue and hid it, keeping it all for himself.

Qunguliq immediately knew why the man had fallen ill. He had broken an ancient taboo by not sharing the polar bear tongue and selfishly eating it all himself.

Having received the truth of the man's illness, Supijaq and Qunguliq made their way out of the underworld and back into the sick man's qarmaq. Qunguliq again confronted him. When he finally confessed to the taboo he had broken, he was able to be healed.

As Supijaq and Qunguliq travelled back to their camp, Supijaq thought about all she had seen.

Back in their qarmaq, Qunguliq sat next to the qulliq, her face lit by the flickering flame.

"So, my apprentice," Qunguliq said, "what have you learned from your trip underground?"

The qarmaq was filled with the howling of the wind just beyond its walls.

Supijaq sat silently, considering her response.

Glossary

Notes on Inuktitut Pronunciation

There are some sounds in Inuktitut that may be unfamiliar to English speakers. The pronunciations below convey those sounds in the following ways:

- A double vowel (e.g., aa, ee) lengthens the vowel sound.
- Capitalized letters denote the emphasis for each word.
- q is a "uvular" sound, a sound that comes from the very back of the throat. This is distinct from the sound for k, which is the same as a typical English "k" sound (known as a "velar" sound).
- ll is a rolled "l" sound.

Inuktitut Term	Pronunciation	Meaning
amauti	a-MOW-ti	a woman's parka with a pouch for carrying a child
iglu	IG-loo	snow house
Kannaaluk	kan-NAA-look	one of the many names for the spirit that controls the sea mammals
qamutiik	qa-mu-TEEK	sled
qarmaq	QAR-maq	sod house
qulliq	QUL-liq	seal oil lamp
Qunguliq	qu-NGU-liq	name
qurvik	QUR-vik	bed pan
Supijaq	su-PI-jaq	name

For additional Inuktitut-language resources, please visit inhabitmedia.com/inuitnipingit.

Born in 1957 in a sod house on Baffin Island, Zacharias Kunuk was a carver in 1981 when he sold three sculptures in Montreal to buy a home video camera and 27" TV to bring back to Igloolik, a settlement of 500 Inuit who had voted twice to refuse access to outside television. After working six years for the Inuit Broadcasting Corporation as producer and station manager, Kunuk co-founded Igloolik Isuma Productions Inc. in 1990 with Paul Apak Angilirq, Pauloosie Qulitalik, and Norman Cohn, and Kunuk Cohn Productions Inc. in 2004 with Norman Cohn. In 2001, Kunuk's first feature, *Atanarjuat: The Fast Runner*, won the Camera d'Or at the Cannes Film Festival and was shown around the world. Kunuk has directed more than thirty films and videos that have screened in film festivals and theatres, museums and art galleries, and on TV. He has honorary doctorates from Trent University and Wilfrid Laurier University and is the winner of the Cannes Camera d'Or, three Genie Awards (including Best Director and Best Picture), a National Arts Award, the National Aboriginal Achievement Award, and the 2017 Technicolor Clyde Gilmour Award from the Toronto Film Critics Association. Zacharias Kunuk was named an Officer of the Order of Canada in 2002.

Megan Kyak-Monteith is an Inuk illustrator and painter born in Pond Inlet, Nunavut. She is currently living in Halifax, Nova Scotia, and studying interdisciplinary arts at NSCAD University with a focus on painting. When she is not working on illustrations, she can be found watching movies with her friends, shopping, or working in her studio on her large-scale oil paintings.

INHABIT
MEDIA